Ten Little FINGERS and Ten Little TOES

MEM FOX

HELEN OXENBURY

Harcourt, Inc.

Orlando Austin New York San Diego London

E
FOX

Library of Congress Cataloging-in-Publication Data

Fox, Mem, 1946–

Ten little fingers and ten little toes/Mem Fox; [illustrations by] Helen Oxenbury.

p.   cm.

Summary: Rhyming text compares babies born in different places and in different circumstances,
but they all share the commonality of ten little fingers and ten little toes.

[1. Babies—Fiction.   2. Fingers—Fiction.   3. Toes—Fiction.   4. Stories in rhyme.]

I. Oxenbury, Helen, ill.   II. Title.

PZ8.3.F8245Te   2008

[E]—dc22   2007010692

ISBN 978-0-15-206057-2

First edition

H G F E D C B A

Manufactured in China

For Helena, who teaches them all
—M. F.

For all the babies of the world
—H. O.

There was one little baby
who was born far away.

And another who was born
on the very next day.

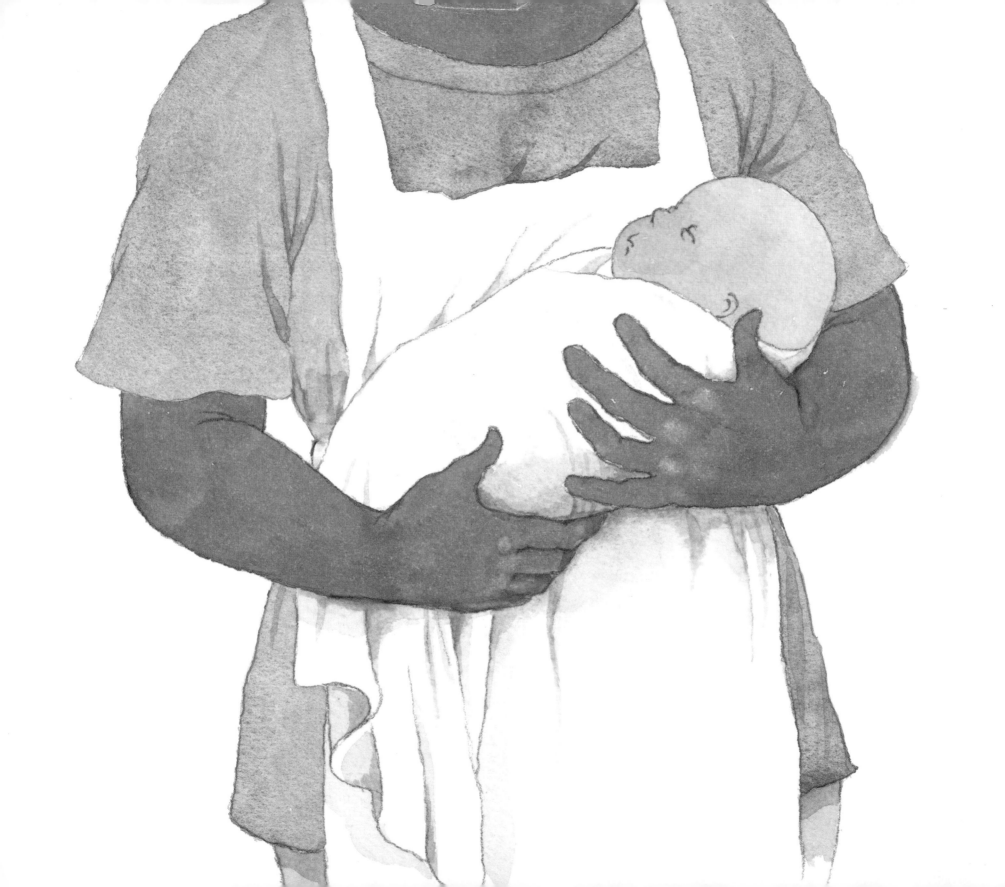

And both of these babies,

as everyone knows,

had ten little fingers

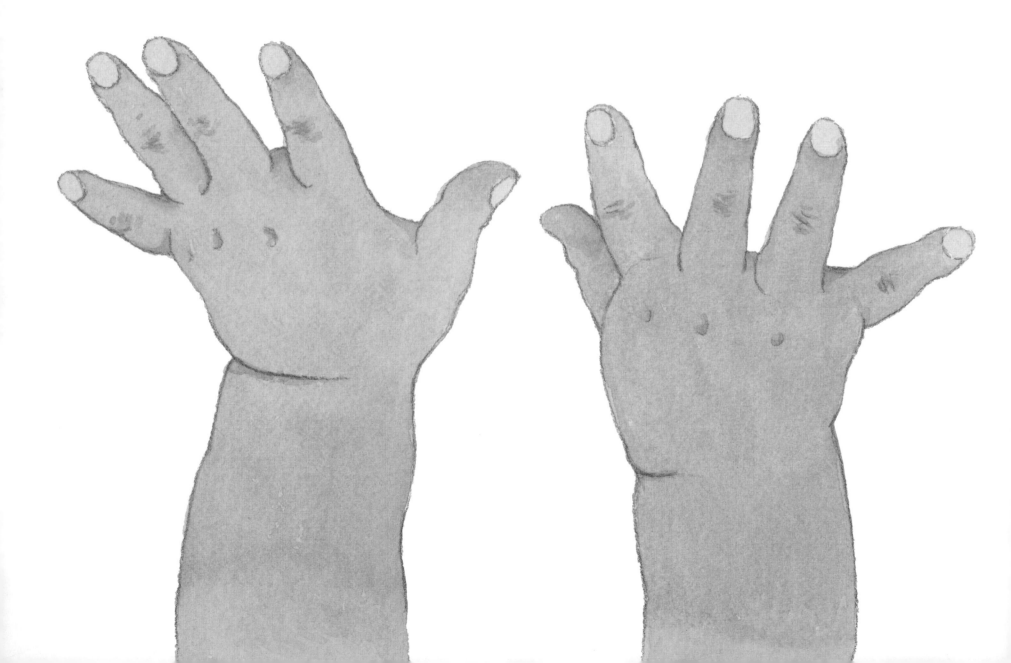

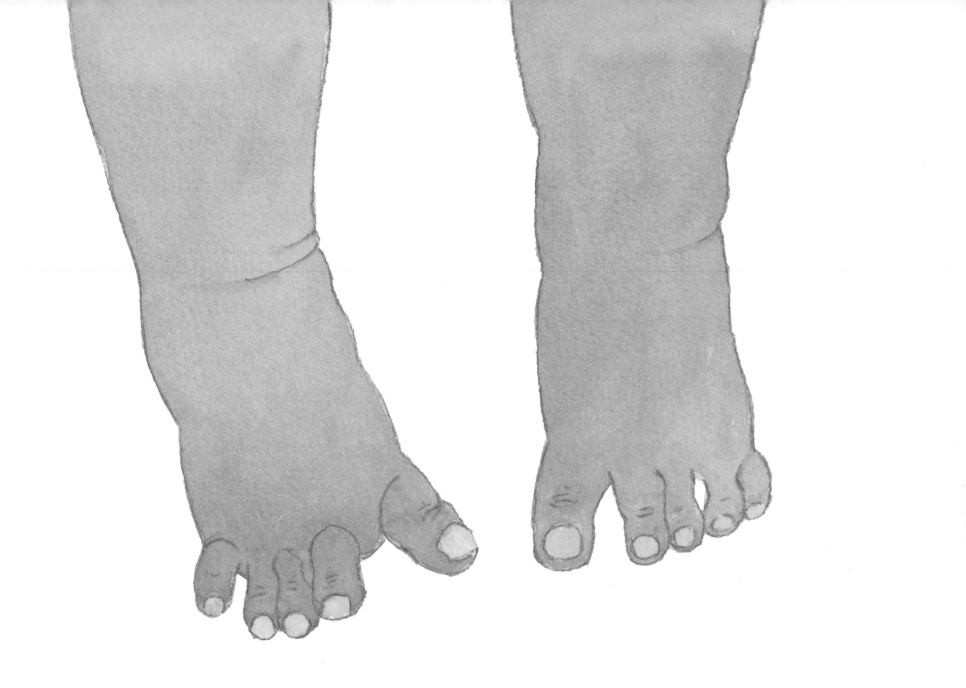

and ten little toes.

There was one little baby who was born in a town.

And another who was wrapped in an eiderdown.

And both of these babies,

as everyone knows,

had ten little fingers

and ten little toes.

There was one little baby
who was born in the hills.

And another who suffered from sneezes and chills.

And both of these babies,

as everyone knows,

had ten little fingers

and ten little toes.

There was one little baby who was born on the ice.

And another in a tent, who was just as nice.

And both of these babies,

as everyone knows,

had ten little fingers

and ten little toes.

But the next baby born was truly divine,
a sweet little child who was mine, all mine.

And this little baby,

as everyone knows,

has ten little fingers,

ten little toes,

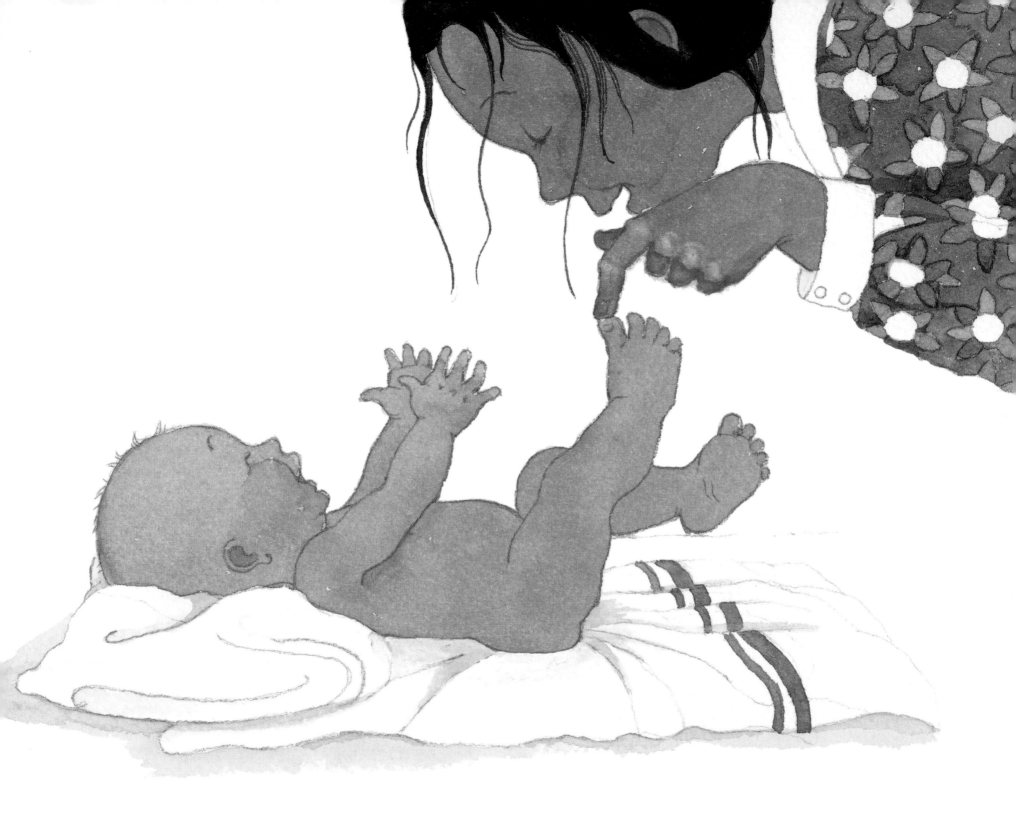

on the tip of its nose.

and three little kisses